W9-BUJ-271

Mr. Marble's Moose

Copyright © 1992 by Debra May Hejtmanek for the text.
Copyright © 1992 by Sabra Smith for the illustrations.

All rights reserved. No portion of this book may be reproduced in any form without the written permission of the publisher, with the exception of brief quotations in reviews.

Managing Editor: Laura Minchew
Project Editor: Brenda Ward

Library of Congress Cataloging-in-Publication Data

Hejtmanek, Debra May
  Mr. Marble's Moose / written by Debra May Hejtmanek ; illustrated by Sabra
Smith.
   p. cm.
  "Word kids!"
  Summary: Three adventures of Mr. Marble and his moose, Sam, who loves to sing loudly.
  ISBN 0-8499-0969-4
  [1. Moose—Fiction. 2. Christian life—Fiction.]
  I. Smith, Sabra, 1961-   ill. II. Title. III. Title: Mister Marble's moose.
  PZ7.M4508Mr 1991

[E]—dc20   92-28921
                                                                  CIP
                                                                   AC

Printed in the United States of America
2 3 4 5 6 7 8 9 R R D 9 8 7 6 5 4 3 2 1

Mr. Marble's Moose

D.J. May

Illustrated by Sabra Smith

E
MAY

WORD PUBLISHING

Dallas · London · Vancouver · Melbourne

GRACE COMMUNITY
CHURCH LIBRARY

To Andrew and Bethany Hejtmanek,
who have taught me the importance
of joyful noise
and silly dreams
about mooses and worms
and other such things.

—D.J.M.

───────────────────

To my dear parents, Bob and Sue Smith
who have offered a lifetime of love, support
and encouragement.

—S.S.

Table of Contents

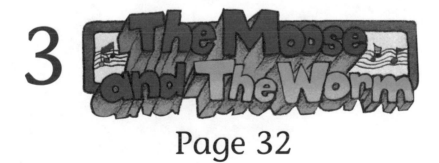

Mr. Marble's Moose

Makes a Joyful Noise

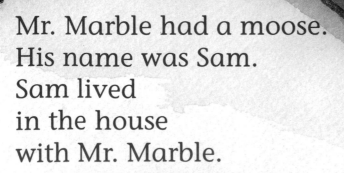

Mr. Marble had a moose.
His name was Sam.
Sam lived
in the house
with Mr. Marble.

Sam loved to sing.
He would sing
and sing
 and sing
  all day long.
Mr. Marble did not mind.

Sam sang songs
about happy things.
At the breakfast table,
he sang about flowers.

During dinner,
he sang about birds.

In the bathtub,
Sam sang about
butterflies and worms.
Sam never sang softly.
He always sang
at the top of his voice.

Mr. Marble sat in his chair
and read the paper.
He did not mind
if Sam sang all day.
Mr. Marble put plugs in his ears.

Sam was full of joy.
He loved God.
He wanted to sing about God.
So he did . . .
even when he mowed the front yard.

But Sam had one little problem.
Dogs howled when he sang
because he never sang
the right notes.
When Sam sang,
it sounded like noise.

Did Sam care?
Not one bit.
He even sang while
he jogged down the street.

Did Mr. Marble care?
Not at all—
at least not when
he had plugs in his ears.

Did God care?
No way.
Mr. Marble read the Bible to Sam.
He read, "Make a joyful noise
unto the Lord."
So Sam did.

The Moose Is Loose

One day Mr. Marble's moose Sam
rode his bicycle
up and down the street
for hours.

He sang all the way up the street.

He sang all the way down the street.
Sam was glad to be alive.

Mrs. Ivy lived across the street
in the yellow house.
She called Mr. Marble
on the telephone.

"Your moose is loose,
and he is singing very loudly,"
she said.
"My dog is howling,
and my cat
is running in circles."
"Oh dear," said Mr. Marble.

Mr. Lark the barber
called Mr. Marble on the telephone.
"Your moose is loose.
He just rode by my shop.
His loud singing broke my window,"
he said.

"Oh dear,"
said Mr. Marble.
He put on his hat
to go find Sam.

On the front porch,
Mr. Marble met a man.
He did not know him.
"Do you have a moose?" the man asked.
"Yes," said Mr. Marble.

"Your moose is loose.
His singing is keeping me awake,"
the man said.
"I work all night.
I sleep all day.
Please make your moose be quiet,"
the man said.

Mr. Marble walked down the street
looking for Sam.
He did not see him,
but he heard him.
He smiled.
Mr. Marble was glad Sam was a happy moose.

Sam rode around the corner
on his bicycle.
He almost knocked
Mr. Marble down.
Sam stopped singing.
"I'm sorry," Sam said.

"Sam, sit under this tree with me," said Mr. Marble.

He told Sam he had been singing too loudly.
He told Sam about Mrs. Ivy's pets.
He told Sam about the barber's window.
He told Sam about the man who could not sleep.

GRACE COMMUNITY CHURCH LIBRARY

Mr. Marble and Sam
walked home.
Sam pushed his bicycle.
He did not sing.

When they got home,
Mr. Marble read to Sam
from the Bible.
He read,
"Be kind to each other…
putting other people's needs
before your own."

Sam thought and thought.
*How can I make a
joyful noise
and be kind to others too?*
Sam had an idea.

Sam was soon
the cleanest moose in town.
Every day,
Sam sang loudly in the shower
for hours and hours.

When he wasn't in the shower,
he sang in the house,
but not at the top of his lungs.

When Sam went outside
to play in the yard,
he still sang.
But he sang very softly.

When he jogged around the block
or rode his bicycle
up and down the street,
he sang.
But he did not sing out loud.
Sam sang inside his heart.

Everyone knew Sam was happy.
A smile was on his big moose face.

The Moose and The Worm

Mr. Marble woke up.
Something was wrong this morning.
He went into the kitchen.
Maybe some toast was burning.
No, that was not it.

Maybe I have lost my hat,
Mr. Marble thought.
He looked under the bed.
He looked in the closet.

He looked in the mirror.
No, his hat was not lost.
It was on his head.

Mr. Marble heard the cars
driving down the road.
He heard a jet
roar in the sky.
He heard a bird
singing outside the window.

Singing!
That's what was wrong.
Sam the Moose was not singing.
Mr. Marble was worried.
Sam always sang in the house.

Mr. Marble looked for Sam
in the bathroom.
Sam was not there.
Mr. Marble looked for Sam
in the washing machine.
Sam was not there.

Mr. Marble looked in the dining room.
Sam was not there.
Mr. Marble looked under the kitchen sink.
Sam was not there either.

Mr. Marble looked outside.
Sam was there.
Sam was sitting on the grass
by the flower garden.
His moose nose
was almost in the dirt.

"What are you looking at?"
asked Mr. Marble.
"A worm," said Sam.
The worm inched across the dirt
away from Sam
very quickly.

"Go away," the worm cried.
"Leave me alone!"
The worm did not like Sam.
This moose was too big.

"I do not like this worm,"
said Sam.
"I wanted to be friends,
but this worm is mean."

Mr. Marble thought this was funny.
A moose wanted to be friends
with a worm?
Mr. Marble tried not to laugh,
but he laughed and laughed and laughed.
Mr. Marble did not think
it was possible
for a moose and a worm
to like each other.

Sam wanted to prove
Mr. Marble was wrong.
A worm and a moose
could be friends.

Sam made up a song.
In the moonlight,
Sam sang the song
to the worm in the garden.

"Worms are wonderful.
Worms dig in the dirt.
I would never go fishing
for a hooked worm would hurt,"
Sam sang softly
with one knee on the earth.

The worm popped his head
out of the dirt.
"You are okay," said the worm
to the moose.

Sam bowed his antlers
down to the ground.
The worm climbed aboard.

The next morning at breakfast,
Sam sat down to eat his eggs.
"Mr. Marble," Sam said,
"Please meet my friend Worm."
The worm wiggled and giggled
on top of Sam's head.

Mr. Marble dropped
his orange juice on the floor.
"All things are possible
with God," Sam sang.
"That's found in the Bible."

Mr. Marble agreed.
Sam was right.
The moose and the worm
were friends for a long time.
Worm lived in the garden
and Sam sang to him
day and night.

E
MAY

AUTHOR May, D.J.

TITLE Mr. Marble's Moose

DATE DUE

E
MAY

May, D.J.

Mr. Marble's Moose

GRACE COMMUNITY
CHURCH LIBRARY